"I will take photos of Bear,"

said Dad.

Amy put Bear on her skateboard.

Dad took a photo of him.

But the skateboard went too fast.

"Oh no!" cried Amy. "Poor Bear!"

Dad picked him up.

Amy got a balloon
and tied it to Bear.
She let go
and Bear went up.

Dad took a photo of him.

But the balloon popped.

Bear fell down into the tree.

"Oh no!" cried Amy. "Poor Bear!"

Dad climbed the tree to get him.

"Thanks, Dad," said Amy.

Amy put Bear in a boat.

She took it to the pond.

Dad took a photo of him.

But the boat started to sink.

"Oh no!" cried Amy. "Poor Bear!"

Dad pulled him out.

"Thanks, Dad," said Amy.

Amy took Bear home.

She showed him to Mum.

"Poor Bear," said Amy.

"He is wet and dirty and ripped."

"I will mend him," said Mum.

"Then you can wash him."

Mum mended Bear.

Then Amy washed him
and hung him up to dry.

"That's better!" she said.

Dad took a photo of Bear.

Amy took Bear back to school.
She showed the photos
to the class.

"Bear had fun," she said.

"But I don't think Dad did."

Story trail

Start

Start at the beginning of the story trail. Ask your child to retell the story in their own words, pointing to each picture in turn to recall the sequence of events.

Independent Reading

This series is designed to provide an opportunity for your child to read on their own. These notes are written for you to help your child choose a book and to read it independently.

In school, your child's teacher will often be using reading books which have been banded to support the process of learning to read. Use the book band colour your child is reading in school to help you make a good choice. *Poor Bear* is a good choice for children reading at Green Band in their classroom to read independently.

The aim of independent reading is to read this book with ease, so that your child enjoys the story and relates it to their own experiences.

About the book

It is Amy's turn to take Bear home and she is very excited. Dad promises to take pictures of their adventures. But Bear gets into all sorts of mishaps and Dad has to come to the rescue.

Before reading

Help your child to learn how to make good choices by asking: "Why did you choose this book? Why do you think you will enjoy it?" Look at the cover together and ask: "What do you think the story will be about?" Support your child to think of what they already know about the story context. Read the title aloud and ask: "What do you think Bear is doing on the cover of the book? What do you think will happen next?"

Remind your child that they can try to sound out the letters to make a word if they get stuck.

Decide together whether your child will read the story independently or read it aloud to you.

During reading

If reading aloud, support your child if they hesitate or ask for help by telling the word. Remind your child of what they know and what they can do independently.

If reading to themselves, remind your child that they can come and ask for your help if stuck.

After reading

Support comprehension by asking your child to tell you about the story. Use the story trail to encourage your child to retell the story in the right sequence, in their own words.

Help your child think about the messages in the book that go beyond the story and ask: "Do you think Bear had fun? Why/why not?" Give your child a chance to respond to the story: "Did you have a favourite part? Do you have a toy that you have adventures with?"

Extending learning

Help your child understand the story structure by using the same sentence patterning and adding different elements. "Let's make up a new story about a toy that has lots of adventures. What will your toy be? What might your toy get up to? Does anyone need to rescue it?" In the classroom, your child's teacher may be looking at adding the suffix -ed to words. Look together at some of the words ending in -ed in this book, for example: *wanted, popped, climbed, ripped, mended, showed, washed, pulled, started.* Ask: "What can you notice about the -ed sound at the end of these words?" Read the words aloud, and point out that the 'ed' sounds different in the range of words.

Franklin Watts
First published in Great Britain in 2017
by The Watts Publishing Group

Copyright © The Watts Publishing Group 2017

Series Editors: Jackie Hamley and Melanie Palmer
Series Advisors: Dr Sue Bodman and Glen Franklin
Series Designer: Peter Scoulding

A CIP catalogue record for this book is
available from the British Library.

ISBN 978 1 4451 5447 3 (hbk)
ISBN 978 1 4451 5448 0 (pbk)
ISBN 978 1 4451 6097 9 (library ebook)

Printed in China

Franklin Watts
An imprint of
Hachette Children's Group
Part of The Watts Publishing Group
Carmelite House
50 Victoria Embankment
London EC4Y 0DZ

An Hachette UK Company
www.hachette.co.uk

www.franklinwatts.co.uk